Monkeys in the Jungle
Angie Sage

hello

from animals
by Lauren Sage

H O U G H T O N   M I F F L I N   C O M P A N Y   B O S T O N

Atlanta   Dallas   Geneva, Illinois   Palo Alto   Princeton   Toronto

Houghton Mifflin Edition, 1991

Printed in the U.S.A.

ISBN: 0-395-53927-7

CDEFGHIJ-FL-998765432

monkey

snake

elephant

parrot

rabbit

ant

hippo

bat

giraffe

4

tiger

bear

goat

fish

crocodile

frog

turtle

lion

penguin

Here are all the animals
Walking in a row

Now they all are going home
Let's see where they go

There are monkeys in the jungle

There are hippos by the pool

There are tigers in the grasslands

And Lions keeping cool

There are crocodiles in the river

There are elephants on the plain

And frogs out in the rain

There are rabbits in their burrows

There are snakes upon the sand

There are parrots in the treetops

And ants march overland

There are goats up in the mountains

There are bats down in the caves

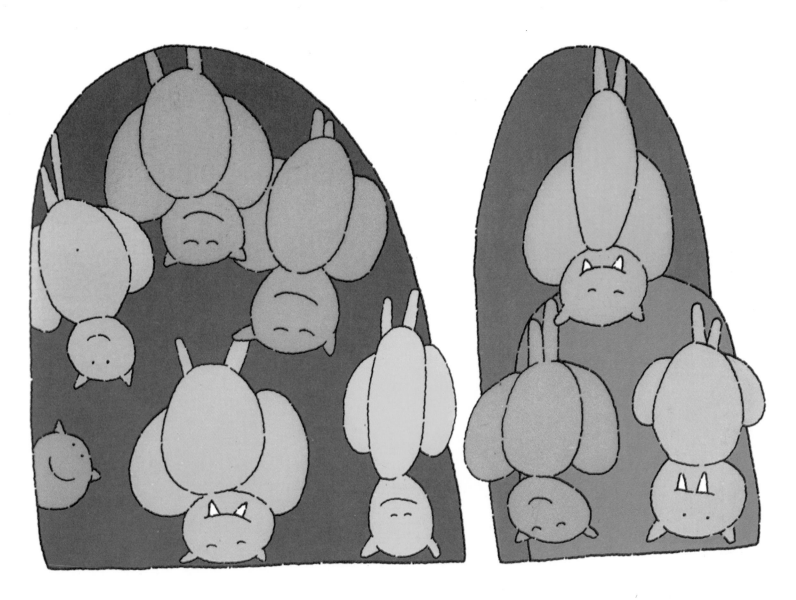

There are bears deep in the forest

And turtles in the waves

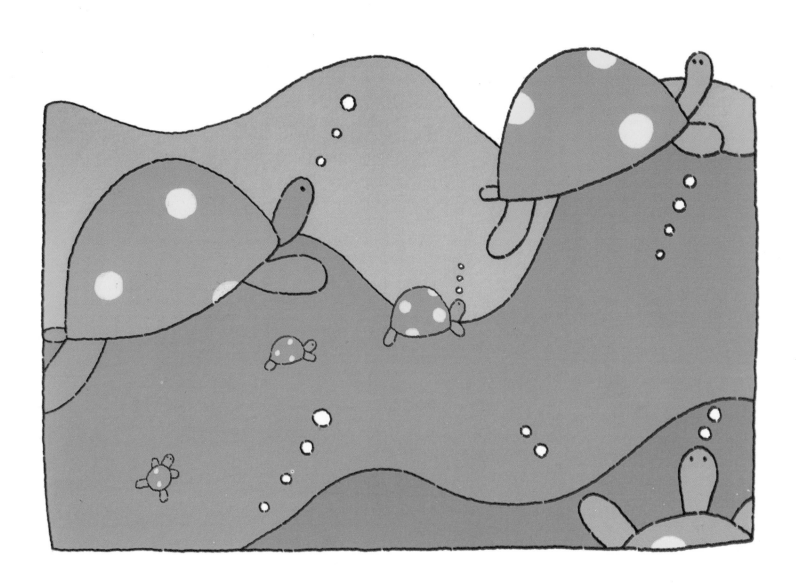

There are penguins on the ice floes

There are fishes in the sea

Now they all are hiding
How many can you see ?